GREAT ILLUSTRATED CLASSICS

A CHRISTMAS CAROL

Charles Dickens

adapted by
Malvina G. Vogel

Illustrations by
Pablo Marcos Studio

BARONET
B·O·O·K·S

BARONET BOOKS, New York, New York

GREAT ILLUSTRATED CLASSICS

edited by
Malvina G. Vogel

Contents

About the Author

Charles Dickens created some of the most famous characters in English literature, for he had a great understanding of the poor and helpless. It is these characters that keep people of all ages reading his books today, more than a hundred years after they were written.

Dickens was born in Portsmouth, in southern England, on February 7, 1812, but his father, a poor clerk, moved his family to London soon afterward. Charles attended school on and off until he was fourteen, taking time off to work in a factory to help support his family. But even after he had to leave school, Charles enjoyed reading books and studying people.

As a newspaper reporter in the 1820s, Dickens developed his writing skills, and in 1836, he became famous for his first major work, *The Pickwick Papers*. During the next four years, Dickens published *Oliver Twist, Nicholas Nickelby, The Old Curiosity Shop,* and *Barnaby Rudge.* Then came his five "Christmas books." The first, in 1843, was *A Christmas Carol*, which has since become Dickens' most widely read tale and one of the most famous stories ever written. Even the name of its main character, Scrooge, has become a commonly used word to describe a miserly person.

Charles Dickens not only enjoyed writing, but also touring the world, giving dramatic readings of his works. Although he became a wealthy man, Dickens worked hard for many charities to help the poor unfortunates he described in many of his books. He continued these activities until his death on June 9, 1870.

Ebenezer Scrooge Signs the Papers.

CHAPTER 1

Ebenezer Scrooge

Jacob Marley was dead. Everyone knew that. There was no doubt about that. All the official papers were properly signed by witnesses to make them legal. The clergyman signed the papers. The city clerk signed them. And the undertaker signed them. Even Ebenezer Scrooge signed them, and everyone knew that anything Scrooge signed had to be perfectly legal!

Yes, Marley was as dead as a doornail.

Did Scrooge know he was dead? Of course he did. How could he not know? After all,

Scrooge and Marley had been business partners for many years. Besides, Scrooge was the executor of Marley's estate, as decreed in his will. Scrooge was Marley's only friend, his only mourner, and the only beneficiary of his estate. Still, Scrooge was an excellent business man and even on the day of Marley's death, he took advantage of the sad event by offering his customers special bargains.

Yes, Scrooge knew without a doubt that Marley was dead, but for some reason, which no one knew, he never painted old Marley's name out of the sign that stood above their warehouse door. It still read, "Scrooge and Marley."

But Scrooge was a tight-fisted old man, squeezing every penny out of a bargain, showing no mercy to those who owed him money, and wrenching every minute of work out of his employees. Yes, he was a cold, solitary old man—cold inside and cold outside. His cold heart froze every feature about

The Scrooge and Marley Warehouse

him—his pointed nose, his shriveled cheeks, his red eyes, his thin blue lips, his wiry chin, and his harsh, grating voice. He even kept everything around him cold; his office was as cold as ice and never felt the slightest warmth, not even at Christmas.

But neither heat nor cold bothered Scrooge. Neither did people. Nobody ever smiled at him in the streets. Nobody ever asked, "My dear Scrooge, how are you?" Nobody ever offered, "Why don't you visit us?" No beggars came up to him to plead for a trifle. No children ever asked him what time it was. No man or woman ever came up to him to ask directions. Even blind men's dogs led their masters off into doorways and up side streets when they saw Scrooge coming.

And did Scrooge care?...No! He actually liked this. He went through life warning all people to keep away from him!

Even a Blind Man's Dog Avoids Scrooge.

Scrooge Is Busy at Work.

CHAPTER 2

Visitors to the Warehouse

It was the afternoon of Christmas Eve and old Scrooge sat busy at work in his office. It was a cold, foggy, bleak day, and Scrooge could hear people in the street outside breathing heavily and stamping their feet on the stone pavement to keep warm. Even though it was only three o'clock, it was already dark, and candles were beginning to appear in the windows of nearby offices.

The fog outside was so thick that it seemed to seep into the office through every keyhole and every slight opening in the walls.

A Christmas Carol

The door to Scrooge's office was open so that he could keep an eye on his clerk writing letters in his tiny office. In Scrooge's own office, a small fire burned, but the one in the clerk's office was so much smaller that it seemed to have only one coal burning. Still, the poor clerk couldn't refuel the fire for Scrooge kept the coal-box in his own office, and even threatened to fire the young man if he dared come in to ask for more. So Bob Cratchit, the clerk, tried to warm himself at the candle that burned at his table, but he did not succeed.

Suddenly, a voice interrupted Scrooge in the midst of his work.

"A Merry Christmas, Uncle!" came a cheerful voice. It was old man Scrooge's nephew, Fred—a handsome young man with sparkling eyes and a glowing face.

"Bah!" said Scrooge, without lifting his head. "Humbug!"

"Christmas a humbug, Uncle!" said the

"A Merry Christmas, Uncle!"

young man. "You can't meant that?"

"I do," said Scrooge. "*Merry* Christmas, indeed! What right do *you* have to be merry? You're poor!"

"Come, Uncle," said Fred, gaily. "What right do *you* have to be grouchy? You're rich!"

And since Scrooge had no answer at the moment, he said, "Bah!" and followed it with "Humbug!"

"Don't be cross, Uncle!" said Fred.

"What else should I be," said Scrooge, "when I live in a world filled with fools? What's so merry about Christmas? It's a time for paying bills when you don't have any money; it's a time when you're a year older and not a penny richer. If I had my way, every fool who goes around saying 'Merry Christmas' would be boiled in his own Christmas pudding! Why, I wouldn't care if Christmas never ever came again!"

"Uncle!" cried his nephew. "What a dreadful thing to say! Christmas means so

"What's So Merry About Christmas?"

much. First, it is a sacred religious time. And then, too, it is a time for forgiving, a time to be charitable and pleasant. It is the only time when people seem to think of others so freely and open up their hearts to each other."

From the other office came the sound of the clerk applauding. Then, realizing immediately what he had done, Bob Cratchit busied himself poking at the remaining coal in the fire and extinguishing the last spark.

"If I hear another sound from you," Scrooge called out to his clerk, "you'll celebrate Christmas by looking for a new job."

"Don't be angry, Uncle," said Fred. "I simply came to invite you to have Christmas dinner with us tomorrow."

"Why, I would rather see you down below with the Devil first than come to your home!"

"But why, Uncle? Why?"

"Why did you get married?"

"Because I fell in love."

"Because you fell in love!" growled Scrooge.

Bob Cratchit Applauds Fred's Words.

"Bah! That's the only thing in the world more ridiculous than a Merry Christmas. Now, leave me, sir. Good afternoon."

"But, Uncle, you never even came to see me *before* I was married. Why are you giving my marriage as a reason for not coming?"

"I said good afternoon," said Scrooge sternly.

"I am truly sorry from the bottom of my heart, Uncle. We have never had a quarrel. I have tried to keep the spirit of Christmas and I will to the end. So, Merry Christmas, Uncle!"

"Good-bye! said Scrooge.

"And a Happy New Year!" called Fred.

"Good-bye!"

Fred left the room, still smiling. He stopped at the outer door to wish a Merry Christmas to Bob Cratchit, who returned the greeting as he let the young man out the door.

At that moment, two rather stout gentlemen, with books and papers in their hands, appeared at that same door, asking to see

Scrooge Refuses Fred's Invitation.

Scrooge. Bob Cratchit showed them into Scrooge's office.

They bowed as a greeting to Scrooge.

One of the men consulted his list and asked, "Is this Scrooge and Marley's?"

Scrooge nodded.

"And am I speaking to Mr. Scrooge or Mr. Marley?" continued the man.

"Mr. Marley has been dead for seven years," answered Scrooge. "In fact, seven years ago tonight."

"Well, then I am certain that you, as his partner, Mr. Scrooge, will want to be as *generous* as he was in donating to the charity we represent."

Upon hearing the word "generous," Scrooge shook his head, for he knew that Marley was no more generous than he was.

But the man seemed to pay no mind to Scrooge's negative shake of his head, and he took up a pen from Scrooge's desk and explained, "At this festive time of the year, we

Requesting a Donation

try to help the poor and destitute who are suffering. There are many thousands who do not have even the bare necessities of life, sir."

"Bah!" replied Scrooge. "There are prisons and workhouses to take care of these people, and laws made by the government to see to their welfare. As far as I am concerned, the government is looking after them well enough."

"But, sir," said the man, "we wish to bring a little extra cheer to these unfortunates. We are raising money to buy some food and drink and a little warmth. At this time of the year, everyone rejoices in giving. Now, how much of a donation may I put you down for?"

"Nothing!" replied Scrooge.

"Ah, you wish your gift to be anonymous?" asked the gentleman, smiling.

"I wish to be left alone," said Scrooge. "I do not consider Christmas merry and I have no desire to make, idle, worthless people merry. Their welfare is not my problem. I have my

Scrooge Refuses!

own business to attend to and I do not concern myself with other people's business. Now, good afternoon, gentlemen."

"But, sir, ..." began the gentleman, "there is never enough government support for these poor people, and many will die!"

"Bah! Humbug!" exclaimed Scrooge. "Then let them die! We already have enough of a surplus population of these wretched creatures anyhow!"

Realizing that they could do nothing to move the old man, the two gentlemen left, and Scrooge returned to his work, feeling quite pleased with himself.

Meanwhile, the fog and darkness had thickened outside and the cold had become more intense. In the street across from the warehouse, some workmen who had been repairing a gas line in the road had lit a fire in a bucket, and a group of ragged men and boys gathered round it to warm their hands. The dancing fire and their good spirits soon

Warming Their Hands at the Fire

prompted one old man, his voice cracking, to sing the first few bars of "God Rest You, Merry Gentlemen." Soon, other voices from these ragged men and boys joined in.

One young lad, his nose frozen and numb from the cold, left the group and crossed the street to the Scrooge and Marley Warehouse. He stooped down at Scrooge's keyhole to sing some lines of the Christmas carol to him. But at the first sound of

God rest you, merry gentlemen,
May nothing you dismay,

Scrooge seized his ruler and shook it toward his closed door so violently that the singer jumped back from the keyhole and fled in terror.

By now, it was closing-time at the warehouse. Scrooge got down off his stool and announced it to Cratchit.

The clerk immediately blew out his candle and took his hat and long woolen scarf down from the hook.

A Caroler at Scrooge's Keyhole

"And I suppose you'll want tomorrow off?" said Scrooge to the young man.

"If it is convenient for you, sir."

"It is *not* convenient," said Scrooge, "and it is not fair either. If I was to dock you a day's wages from your pay, you'd think I was being unfair, wouldn't you?"

The clerk smiled weakly.

"And yet," continued Scrooge, "you don't think it unfair that I should pay you a day's wages for no work."

"But it's only once a year, sir," pleaded Cratchit.

"Yes, once a year—every twenty-fifth of December!" said Scrooge. "It's a poor excuse for picking a man's pocket, making me pay you for staying home! Well then, Cratchit, you'd better be here earlier on the following morning."

"Oh, yes, sir," promised the young man.

With that, Scrooge buttoned up his coat, slammed on his hat, and walked out growling.

"I Suppose You'll Want Tomorrow Off?"

A Melancholy Dinner

CHAPTER 3

Marley's Ghost

Scrooge stopped at his usual tavern, took his usual table, and ate his usual melancholy dinner. No other customers greeted him and he greeted none of them. He passed the time reading all his newspapers and checking his bankbooks. And when all the papers had been read and all the bankbooks checked, Scrooge went home to bed.

Scrooge lived in the apartment that once belonged to his partner, Jacob Marley. It was a gloomy old place in a small building that was now surrounded by other, larger ones.

A Christmas Carol

The building was such a dreary one that no one chose to live there. So the other rooms were rented out as offices.

The front courtyard was dark in the fog and frost as Scrooge entered the gate and walked to the door. As he inserted the key in the lock, his eye caught a glimpse of the large shiny, brass knocker on the door. It was the same knocker he had been seeing morning and night for all the years he lived in the building. But suddenly, tonight, it was not a knocker that stared back at him from the door...no...it was the face of Jacob Marley!

"But Jacob Marley is dead!" thought Scrooge, frozen to the spot. "My eyes must be playing tricks on me. Just because of those visitors I had this afternoon—those two men seeking charity—my thoughts returned to Marley, quite by chance."

Now Scrooge stared harder at the knocker. Here *was* Marley's face, with a dismal light around it!...Marley's face with ghostly

The Face of Jacob Marley!

spectacles raised on its ghostly forehead...
Marley's face with hair blowing strangely and wildly about his head ...Marley's face with eyes wide open and bulging, but not moving.

As Scrooge stood there, unable to tear his gaze from the door, the strange vision became a knocker again.

"Did I imagine that vision in the knocker?" he asked himself, with his heart thumping nervously.

But since he could find no answer, Scrooge forced himself to turn the key in the lock and walk inside.

Yes, he decided, he must have imagined it all. Still, before he shut the door, he looked carefully behind it as if he half-expected to see Marley. but there was nothing—only the screws and nuts that fastened the knocker to the door.

"Pooh, pooh!" cried Scrooge, slamming the door with a bang. He was angry with himself

Only Screws and Nuts Behind the Door

as he lit his candle and climbed the stairs to his rooms.

Although Scrooge had always liked the darkness, now, as he entered his apartment, it made him remember Marley's face in the knocker. He walked nervously from room to room, first with his candle held high, then poking it into corners and under furniture. Nobody was under the table; nobody was under the sofa; nobody was under the bed; nobody was in the closet. Scrooge even looked inside his dressing-gown as it hung on the hook on the wall. But nobody was inside it either. A small fire was in the grate; a little pot of broth was warming on the fireplace ledge.

Satisfied that he was alone, Scrooge closed and locked his door, which he didn't normally do. Then, taking off his coat and jacket and putting on his dressing-gown, slippers, and nightcap, Scrooge sat down before the fire to eat his broth.

The fire was low—very low for such a bitter

Scrooge Checks Under the Furniture.

night. As Scrooge moved closer to get every bit of warmth from it, he looked at the familiar tiles set into the fireplace around the hearth. He remembered remarking to himself when he had first moved in that the fireplace must have been built by a Dutchman years ago, for the tiles were old Dutch scenes illustrating the Bible. But now these scenes were suddenly gone, and in their place appeared the shape of old Marley's head, staring out at Scrooge from each smooth tile!

"Humbug!" cried Scrooge angrily, as he jumped up and strode across the room.

After a few minutes of pacing, Scrooge returned to the fireside and sat down again. As he leaned his head back against the chair, his eyes were raised and his glance came to rest on a bell. It was a bell that had always been in the room—a bell that had hung there, unused.

Now, suddenly, this long-silent bell began to swing. Scrooge stared, first with astonishment, then with terror. At first, the bell

Marley's Head Stares Out From the Tiles.

swung softly, barely making a sound. But soon it rang out loudly and was followed, almost in a chorus, by every bell in the house!

The ringing may have lasted a minute, but to Scrooge it seemed like an hour. Then, suddenly, the bells stopped.

Just as Scrooge was about to catch his breath, a new sound gripped his heart—a clanking noise from deep down below, as if someone were dragging a heavy chain over the wine casks stored in the basement. With a shudder, Scrooge recalled having heard that ghosts in haunted houses dragged chains and that. . . .

At that moment, Scrooge heard the cellar door fly open with a bang. It was followed by the sound of the dragging chain coming up the stairs. Up, up, closer and closer to his door!

"It's humbug!" cried Scrooge. "I won't believe it."

But no sooner were the angry words out of his mouth than his face went white. His eyes

The Bell Rings Out.

popped and his jaw dropped open in amazement. For coming through the heavy locked door was Jacob Marley, or rather his *Ghost!* There was no doubt, for it was Jacob Marley's pigtail, his usual waistcoat, his tights and boots. And he was dragging a chain that was wound around his waist...but what a strange chain it was—made of cash boxes, keys, padlocks, ledger books, and heavy steel purses. Marley's body was transparent, so that Scrooge, looking at him, could see right through to the two buttons at the rear of his coat. As he raised his head, Scrooge met the death-cold eyes of the Ghost as they stared back at him.

"Well, now," said Scrooge coldly, "what do you want with me?"

"Much!" It *was* Marley's voice!

"Who are you?" demanded Scrooge.

"Ask me who I *was*," replied the Ghost.

"Who *were* you then?"

"In life, I was your partner, Jacob Marley,"

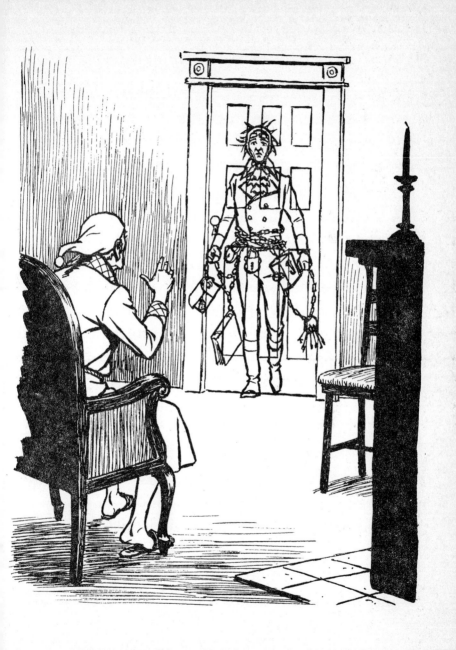

Marley's Ghost Comes Through the Door.

said the Ghost as he sat down in a chair alongside the fireplace. Then he turned to stare directly into Scrooge's eyes and said flatly, "You don't believe in me."

"I don't," said Scrooge.

"What proof do you need that I am real" asked the Ghost. "You see and hear me."

"But my sight and hearing could be affected by an upset stomach, and I *do* suffer from many of them," replied Scrooge. "You may be a bit of undigested beef, or a piece of uncooked potato, or a crumb of cheese, or even a fragment of a toothpick I might have swallowed. Humbug, I tell you! Humbug!"

Hearing this, the Ghost let out a frightful cry and shook his chain with such a horrible noise that Scrooge fell to his knees and buried his face in his hands.

"Have Mercy!" he cried. "I believe in you. Yes! But why have you come to me?"

"The spirit in every man should walk among his fellow men when he is alive," said

A Horrible Noise!

the Ghost. "But if that spirit does not do so during a man's lifetime, it must do it after his death. The spirit must share the unhappiness on earth that he might have been able to turn to happiness when he was alive." And again the Ghost let out a cry and shook his chain.

"Why are you chained?" asked Scrooge.

"It is a chain I, myself, made during my life," said the Ghost. "I made it, link by link, willingly, just as you are now doing. But your chain, Scrooge, is much longer and much heavier than mine, for yours has grown much these last seven years.

Scrooge looked around him on the floor, half-expecting to see yards and yards of iron chains. But he saw nothing.

"Jacob!" he begged. "Jacob Marley, tell me more! Speak to me! Comfort me!"

"I cannot comfort you, Ebenezer Scrooge," said the Ghost. "Comfort is given to other men. Nor can I tell you much more—only that my spirit never thought of my fellow men

"I Made the Chain Myself."

when I was alive. It never walked among them when I was alive. It never left our office when I was alive, never sought out those creatures I might have helped. So now I am destined to roam throughout the world, never to rest and never to have peace. For no matter how I misused my life and no matter how much I regret my selfishness, there is no way for me to make amends!"

"But you were a good business man, Jacob," said Scrooge.

"Business!" cried the Ghost. "My fellow man should have been my business; charity should have been my business; mercy, kindness, and generosity should have been my business. And at this time of year I suffer the most, for I remember all the Christmas times I walked through crowds of my fellow men with my eyes down—never looking up to that Heavenly star that led the Wise Men to a stable so long ago." And again he let out a cry.

Scrooge began to tremble violently.

Marley's Ghost Suffers at Christmas.

A Christmas Carol

"Hear me!" cried the Ghost. "My time is nearly up. I am not allowed to explain to you why you can see me now. But I can tell you that I have sat beside, you, invisible, for many and many a day."

Scrooge shivered and wiped the perspiration from his brow.

"I am here tonight to warn you, Ebenezer that you still have a chance of escaping the same fate as mine."

"You were always my good friend," said Scrooge gratefully. "Thank you!"

"You will be haunted by Three Spirits," continued the Ghost.

"If that is the chance you mentioned, I think I'd rather not."

"Without their visits, you cannot avoid the fate I had. You can expect the first Spirit tomorrow night at one o'clock."

"Couldn't they all come at once and let me be done with it, Jacob?"

The Ghost ignored Scrooge's question.

"You Will Be Haunted by Three Spirits."

A Christmas Carol

"You can expect the second Spirit on the following night, at the same time. And the third will come at the last stroke of twelve on the next night. You will not see me anymore, Ebenezer. But for your own sake, remember all that I have told you."

The Ghost backed away from Scrooge. With each step he took, the window raised itself a little, so that by the time the Ghost had reached it, it was wide open. He beckoned Scrooge to come to him, and when the two were only a step from each other, Marley's Ghost held up his hand.

As Scrooge stopped, he heard strange sounds in the air—cries of sorrow and wails of regret. The Ghost joined in with these sounds as he floated out through the window and into the dark night.

Scrooge rushed to the window and looked out. The air was filled with ghosts, wandering every which way, moaning as they floated. Every one of them wore chains. Scrooge

The Ghost Floats Through the Window.

recognized one of them as a greedy banker he had known. He was now an old ghost with a huge iron safe attached to his ankle. He was floating over a poor woman sitting out in the cold, an infant in her arms. And he was crying pitifully because he did not have the power to help her. It was a power he did have once, but did not use it when he was alive.

Soon the spirits faded away and Scrooge closed the window. He went to the door through which the Ghost had entered and examined it carefully. It was still double-locked, as he had fastened it with his own hands earlier. Scrooge was about to say "Humbug!" but he got no further than "Hum—" when he stopped. Was it because of his conversation with the Ghost? Was it because the hour was late? Or was it because he was terrified of his fate?

Scrooge did not even bother to take off his dressing-gown, but lay down on his bed and fell asleep instantly.

An Old Ghost Cannot Help a Poor Woman.

Scrooge Tries To Figure Out the Time.

CHAPTER 4

The Ghost of Christmas Past

When Scrooge awoke, it was so dark that he could not tell where the walls ended and the windows began. As he was trying to decide what time it was, he heard the neighboring church clock strike twelve.

"Twelve!" cried Scrooge. "Why it was past two o'clock when I went to bed! It isn't possible that I slept through a whole date and into the next night. No it must be twelve noon."

With that, Scrooge scrambled out of bed and groped his way to the window. He rubbed the frost off it with the sleeve of his dressing gown, but all he could see outside was darkness and fog. There were no noises of people in the street as there would be if it were noon.

Scrooge slowly returned to his bed, more confused than ever. The more he thought about the lost time, the more confused he got.

"Marley's Ghost was a dream," he said over and over again, trying to reassure himself. But each time, he'd follow his own words with a question, "Or was it?"

Scrooge lay awake in the darkness while the church chime went three quarters more past the hour. Suddenly, he remembered that Marley's Ghost had warned him of a visit when the clock struck one.

That last quarter hour seemed to take so long that Scrooge almost convinced himself that he had dozed off and missed the one o'clock bell. Then the deep, dull hour bell struck one long tone.

Only Darkness and Fog Outside

A Christmas Carol

Lights suddenly flashed in his room and the curtains of his bed were drawn aside, *by a hand!*

Scrooge sat bolt upright in bed and found himself face to face with the unearthly visitor who had opened the curtains. It was a strange figure—like a child, yet like an old man. Its face was soft and smooth, with no sign of a wrinkle, yet its hair was white and hung down its back. Its arms were long and its hands were strong and muscular. Its legs and feet were bare. A pure white tunic trimmed with summer flowers covered its body, and it held a branch of fresh, green winter holly in one hand. But the strangest of all was the jet of light that shone from the top of its head—a light that lit up everything around it.

"Are you a Spirit, sir, that I was told to expect?" asked Scrooge.

"I am," came a soft, gentle voice. "I am the Ghost of Christmas Past. *Your* past Ebenezer Scrooge."

The Ghost of Chistmas Past

A Christmas Carol

"And why have you come here?"

"For your welfare, Ebenezer Scrooge."

"Why, thank you, Spirit," said Scrooge, who then thought to himself, "but I think a night of undisturbed sleep would be better for my welfare!"

The Spirit, who surely had the power to hear Scrooge's thoughts, then cried out, "Let us proceed with saving you, Ebenezer Scrooge!"

And the ghost put out its strong hand and took Scrooge gently by the arm.

"Rise and walk with me!" it commanded.

Scrooge would have like to argue that the weather and the hour were not appropriate for a walk, that his bed was warm, and that he was wearing only a dressing-gown, slippers, and nightcap. But Scrooge found himself unable to resist that gentle grasp, so he rose and followed the Spirit to the window.

"I am a mortal," cried Scrooge as the Spirit prepared to go out the window. "I shall fall."

Scrooge Cannot Resist the Spirit's Grasp.

"All I need do is touch your *here*," said the Spirit, touching Scrooge's heart, "and you will not fall anywhere!"

As the Spirit spoke these words, the two passed through the closed window and found themselves far away from the city, standing on an open country road. The city had completely vanished. Not a trace of it was to be seen. The fog and darkness had vanished too and it was a clear, cold, wintry day, with snow covering the fields alongside the road.

"Good Heavens!" cried Scrooge. "I was born in this countryside, and grew up here!" And for the next few moments, a thousand thoughts, hopes, joys, and cares of his childhood passed through his head.

"Your lips are trembling," said the Ghost. "And what is that on your cheek?"

"Only a pimple," muttered Scrooge unwilling to admit that it was a tear. "Please Spirit, lead me on."

"Do you remember the way?" asked the Spirit.

"What Is That on Your Cheek?"

A Christmas Carol

"Remember it!" cried Scrooge eagerly. "I could walk it blindfolded."

"Strange, then, that you have forgotten it for so many years!" said the Ghost.

As they walked along the road, Scrooge recognized every gate, every post, every tree. Soon, a little town appeared in the distance, with its bridge, its church, and winding river.

Some ponies came trotting towards them, with boys on their backs calling happily to other boys in carts driven by farmers.

"These are only shadows of things past," said the Ghost. "They cannot see us."

As the merry travelers got closer, Scrooge knew every boy by name.... But why was he so overjoyed to see them? Why did his cold eyes glisten with tears and his heart leap up as the boys went past? Why was he filled with gladness when he heard them wish each other a Merry Christmas? After all, what was merry about Christmas to Ebenezer Scrooge?

Scrooge Knows Every Boy By Name.

A Christmas Carol

"That school up ahead is not quite empty," said the Spirit. "One single child, neglected by his family and friends, is still there."

"I know that," said Scrooge, sobbing. "I know him well."

They turned off the main road into a familiar lane and soon approached a large, red brick building. A weather vane sat on the roof, with a bell hanging from it. The building had seen some very poor days; most of its rooms were now rarely used; its walls were damp and covered with moss; many of its windows were broken; and its gate was rotting. The sheds outside were overrun with grass and chickens strutted through the empty stables.

As Scrooge and the Spirit entered a door off the dreary hall, they saw a bare room, with lines of desks still in position. At a desk sat one lone boy, reading. He had chosen a desk near the weak fire to try to keep warm.

An Old, Familiar School

A Christmas Carol

Scrooge sat down upon a bench and wept to see his long-forgotten self as a boy.

Suddenly, a strange figure appeared outside the schoolroom window. It was a woodcutter, with an ax stuck in his belt. He was leading a donkey loaded down with wood.

"Why, it's Ali Baba!" cried Scrooge joyously. "Dear old Ali Baba came to visit that boy sitting there reading! I remember one Christmas when the boy was left here all alone after his classmates had gone home for the holidays, and Ali Baba came to keep him company. And look! There's the Genie too!"

Was this really Ebenezer Scrooge, laughing and crying, excited over friends he had made in his childhood books—friends who kept him company when he was deserted by live ones?

"And there's the parrot!" cried Scrooge. "Poor Robinson Crusoe! Home again after sailing around his island. And there goes Friday, running towards the creek!"

Friends from Childhood Books

A Christmas Carol

Then Scrooge's voice suddenly took on a tone of pity. "Poor boy!" he said of his former self, and began to weep again. "I wish. . . but it's too late now."

"What do you wish?" asked the Spirit.

"Nothing," said Scrooge, "nothing. There was a boy singing Christmas carols at my door last night. I wish I had given him something, that's all."

The Spirit smiled thoughtfully and waved its hand. "Let us see another Christmas!"

At those words, Scrooge's former self grew taller, and the schoolroom became darker and dirtier. More windows were cracked pieces of plaster had fallen out of the ceiling, more rooms were deserted; and even the chickens no longer strutted through the stables.

And the boy was alone again, when all the other boys had gone home for the holidays.

The boy was not reading now; he was walking up and down in despair.

A Boy Alone Again

A Christmas Carol

Scrooge, watching this, shook his head sadly and glanced toward the door, remembering what was to come.

The door opened and a little girl, much younger than the boy, came darting in. She threw her arms around the boy's neck and kissed him, calling him "dear, dear brother."

"I have come to bring you home, dear brother!" cried the little girl joyfully.

"Home, dear little Fan?" asked the puzzled boy.

"Yes!" cried the girl. "Home for ever and ever. Father is so much kinder now than he used to be. He speaks so gently to me now that one night I got up the courage to ask him if you could come home. And he said yes, you could. And he sent me in a coach to bring you. And we're going to be together all Christmas and have the merriest time in the world!"

Fan clapped her hands and laughed. She stood on tiptoe to hug her brother. And she

"I Have Come To Bring You Home!"

began tugging eagerly at his sleeve, trying to pull him towards the door.

"She was a delicate creature," said the Spirit to Scrooge, "and she had a good heart!"

"Yes, she did," said Scrooge.

"But she died after she was grown, didn't she?" asked the Spirit. "Shortly after she was married and had children?"

"One child," answered Scrooge.

"Yes," said the Spirit. "Your nephew, Fred."

Scrooge seemed uneasy as he answered, "Yes."

Although it was only a moment since they had been in the school during the day, Scrooge and the Spirit were now transported to a busy, lighted city street. It was evening, and shadowy people came and went, and shadowy carts and coaches battled for space in the roads. Looking around him, Scrooge saw from the decorations in the shops that here, too, it was Christmas. He followed the

A Busy City Street

Spirit until its shadowy outline stopped at a warehouse door.

"Do you recognize this?" asked the Ghost.

"Recognize it!" cried Scrooge. "I was apprenticed here."

They went inside and saw an old gentleman sitting on a high stool. It was so high that if it had been two inches taller, the man's head would have hit the ceiling.

"Why, it's old Fezziwig!" cried Scrooge with excitement. "Bless his heart!"

Old Fezziwig laid down his pen and looked up at the clock. Seeing that it was seven, he called out in his jovial voice, "Yo ho, there! Ebenezer! Dick!"

Scrooge's former self, now a grown young man, hurried into the room, followed by his fellow apprentice.

"It's Dick Wilkins, to be sure!" cried Scrooge to the Ghost. "He was very close to

"Yo Ho, There! Ebenezer! Dick!"

me. Wilkins was my good friend."

"Yo, ho, my boys!" cried Fezziwig. "No more work tonight. It's Christmas Eve, my lads! Let's clear away and have lots of room here!" And he skipped down in a single hop from his high desk.

Ebenezer and Dick cleared away the desks and swept and washed the floor, while Mr. Fezziwig heaped more coals on the fire. The warehouse was soon snug, warm, and dry, and bright as a party room.

In came a fiddler, with a music book in hand. When he began to play, his music sounded like fifty stomach aches, but to the boys it was a beautiful orchestra.

In came Mrs. Fezziwig, smiling, followed by the three lovable Miss Fezziwigs and the young men courting them.

In came the men and women who worked in Mr. Fezziwig's warehouse.

In came the housemaid, with her cousin,

Preparing the Warehouse for a Party

the baker.

In came the cook and her friend, the milkman.

In came friends and in came neighbors.

In they all came, one after another—some shyly, some boldly; some gracefully, some clumsily. And, arms about each other, they frolicked and danced to the fiddler's music.

There were cakes and puddings and mince pies and cold beef. And there was hot wine and lots of cold beer.

But the high point of the evening came when Mr. Fezziwig stood up to dance with Mrs. Fezziwig. Despite their age and size, their feet seemed to float on air, as they danced more gracefully and with more energy than couples half their age.

When the clock struck eleven, the party broke up. Mr. and Mrs. Fezziwig stood at the door, shaking hands with each of their guests and wishing them all a Merry Christmas as they left.

Mr. and Mrs. Fezziwig Dance.

A Christmas Carol

When all the guest had gone, the Fezziwigs wished the same Merry Christmas to their two apprentices, and the boys headed for their beds in the back room of the warehouse full of praise for the Fezziwig's.

All the while this party scene was taking place, Scrooge watched and acted as if he were part of it as it was happening. He slapped his hands to the music, licked his lips at the food, nodded happily to the guests, and even held out his hand to say farewell to the Fezziwigs.

"It cost so little," said the Ghost, "to make so many people happy at that party. Fezziwig spent a few pounds—three or four perhaps. Do you really think he deserves all the praise the boys heaped on him?"

"It isn't that," said Scrooge, speaking more like his younger, former self. "Fezziwig has the power to make us happy or unhappy, to make our work a pleasure or a burden. No, Spirit, the happiness Fezziwig gives is as

Hearing the Boys Thank the Fezziwigs

great as if it cost a fortune."

Realizing that the Ghost was staring at him, Scrooge stopped talking.

"What is the matter?" asked the Ghost.

"Nothing, particularly," answered Scrooge. "I was just thinking that I would like to say a kind word or two to my clerk, Bob Cratchit, right now."

But at that moment, Scrooge and the Ghost once again stood side by side in another room. And Scrooge now saw himself as an older man—in his twenties, perhaps, in the prime of his life. But already his face had begun to show the signs of greed and worry. Now Scrooge was not alone. He sat alongside a pretty young girl. Tears were in her eyes as she spoke to Scrooge's former self.

"It doesn't matter to you at all," she said softly, "that another love has replaced me in your heart. And if this love can cheer you and comfort you in the future as I would have

"Another Love Has Replaced Me."

done, then I will not weep and grieve for you."

"Good Heavens, Bell! What love are you talking about?" asked Scrooge. "What love do you say has replaced you in my heart?"

"Gold," she whispered. "For now gold is the only thing you love."

"But this is how the world is," said Scrooge. "Nothing is worse than poverty, yet these very same poor people condemn those who seek wealth."

"But, Ebenezer," protested Bell, "once you had more noble goals in life—goals which you have cast aside so you could concentrate only on gaining money."

"But my feelings toward you have not changed!" cried the young man.

"We pledged our love a long time ago when we were both poor," she reminded him. "And we agreed to wait until our financial situation improved. When you made the pledge, you were a different man. You have changed, Ebenezer."

"My Feelings Have Not Changed!"

"I was a boy then!" he said impatiently. "We all change in some ways."

"But I have not changed," she said sadly, "and so I am releasing you from your promise to marry me."

"I never asked you to do that," he said.

"In words, no," she replied. "But in your changed attitudes, in your changed goals in life, you have asked me that very thing... Tell me, Ebenezer, if we hadn't known each other all these years, would you now seek me for a wife—me, a poor girl with no dowry?"

Scrooge did not reply.

"No, Ebenezer, you would have nothing to gain by marrying me—no gold to make you richer. This is why, because of the Ebenezer Scrooge I once loved, that I now release you from your promise."

The young man started to speak, but the girl turned away from him and continued to speak. "This may cause you some pain for a brief time, but you will forget me just as you

Bell Releases Ebenezer from His Promise.

forget a bad dream. May you be happy in the life you have chosen!"

And she stood up and walked away.

"Ghost!" cried Scrooge. "Do not torture me any more! Take me home!"

"Just one more shadow," said the Ghost.

"No more!" cried Scrooge. "No more! I don't want to see any more."

But the Ghost grasped Scrooge's arms and forced him to gaze upon the scene that was appearing before them.

They were inside a room—not a large luxurious room, but a comfortable one, with a cheerful fire burning in the hearth. Next to the fire sat a beautiful girl who looked much like the girl in the last scene that Scrooge believed that it was the same one... until he saw *her*, Bell, now an attractive matron, sitting opposite her daughter.

The noise in this room was deafening, for

Bell's Happy Family

there were more children than Scrooge could count. But neither mother nor daughter seemed to be bothered about the noise; in fact, they seemed to be enjoying it... even to joining in the children's games.

Now a knocking was heard at the door and all the children rushed toward it, carrying the two laughing women along with them. They all greeted the father, who came home accompanied by a coachman loaded down with toys and Christmas presents.

The children shouted with wonder and delight as each gift was opened. And for a long while afterward, the mother and father beamed happily as the children played with their gifts. Then slowly, the tired children began to leave the parlor and go upstairs to bed.

And now Scrooge watched more closely as the father, with his daughter leaning lovingly on him, sat down with her and her mother at

Greeting Their Father

the fireside. And when Scrooge thought how perhaps that beautiful young girl might have been *his* daughter... might have brought joy to *his* life, his eyes grew full with tears.

"Spirit!" cried Scrooge in a broken voice. "Take me away from here!"

"I told you these were shadows of things that are past," said the Ghost. "They are what they are. I did not make them happen."

"Take me away!" cried Scrooge. "I cannot bear it! Take me back! Stop haunting me!"

With that, Scrooge grabbed the cap hanging down the Ghost's back and quickly pressed it on its head, hoping that by putting out the Ghost's light, he could make it go away. But though Scrooge pressed the cap all the way down to the ground over the invisible figure, the light still shone from under it.

Scrooge felt exhausted and drowsy. Not sooner had he given the cap one last squeeze than he found himself in his own bedroom. He reeled into bed and fell into a heavy sleep.

Scrooge Tries To Put Out the Ghost's Light.

Scrooge Pushes Aside the Curtains.

CHAPTER 5

The Ghost of Christmas Present

Scrooge awakened in the middle of a loud snore. He sat up in bed to clear his head, realizing that the clock would soon be striking one. He knew that something inside him woke him up at that moment so he'd be awake to have his meeting with the second ghost.

Rather than wait and be surprised again by the ghost's opening one of his curtains, Scrooge pushed them all aside himself and lay down again to wait nervously.

"What will this one look like?" muttered Scrooge. "I'm sure I wouldn't be surprised by anything from a baby to a rhinoceros!"

So, prepared for almost anything, Scrooge was surprised when the clock struck one and no ghost appeared. As the minutes went by... five...ten...fifteen...and nothing came he began to tremble. As he lay there, a blaze of light began shining on his bed.

"Perhaps it's coming from the sitting room" thought Scrooge. "I'd better trace it."

So, getting up out of bed softly, Scrooge shuffled in his slippers to the door. The instant his hand touched the knob to turn it, a strange voice called his name.

"Ebenezer Scrooge, enter this room!"

Scrooge obeyed.

It was his own sitting-room, there was no doubt. But it had changed completely. Leaves and branches of holly, mistletoe, and ivy, all covered with berries, hung from the walls and ceiling. A roaring fire blazed in the hearth. And piled on the floor, forming a thronelike couch, were huge roasts of meat, turkeys, and

A Blaze of Light Shines on His Bed.

suckling pigs.; long strings of sausages; and mince pies, plum puddings, apples, oranges, cakes, and bowls of punch.

Seated on this feast throne was a jolly, smiling giant. High above him he held a torch shaped like a Horn of Plenty.

"Come in!" called the Ghost warmly.

Scrooge entered timidly, his head bowed before the Ghost. Although the Ghost's eyes were friendly and kind, Scrooge did not want to meet them.

"Look at me!" said the Spirit. "I am the Ghost of Christmas Present."

Scrooge obeyed. What he saw was a figure dressed in a simple dark green robe trimmed with white fur. It hung loosely around the Spirit's body. Tied around his waist was an ancient rusty sheath, but no sword was in it. The Spirit's feet were bare below the robe. On his head was a holly wreath, set with shining icicles. Dark brown hair hung long and loosely from his head, framing a friendly

The Ghost of Christmas Present

face, sparkling eyes, and a cheery voice.

"You have never seen anything like me before, have you?" asked the Spirit.

"Never," answered Scrooge. "But please, Good Spirit, take me wherever you wish. Last night I was forced to go with the first Spirit and I learned a valuable lesson. Tonight, if you have anything to teach me, I am ready."

"Touch my robe!" commanded the Spirit.

Scrooge obeyed and was instantly stuck to the robe.

And in that same instant, the holly, mistletoe, berries, meat, turkeys, pigs, sausages, pudding, fruit, and punch all vanished too. So did the room, the fire, the glowing light, and the night.

Scrooge and the Spirit now stood on the city streets on Christmas morning. The weather was cold and the sky gloomy. Snow covered everything—white on the rooftop, and gray and black in the road, where carts and wagons made deep burrows. Some people

"Touch My Robe!"

were shoveling snow from the pavement and others were sweeping it from their roofs, much to the delight of children who watched as rooftop snowstorms fell in the road. Even the people on the roofs were having a jolly time calling to each other and even throwing a snowball or two at each other.

The fruit shop was open and baskets of chestnuts and almonds sat at the door. Apples and pears and oranges were piled high in pyramids, and bunches of grapes dangled from hooks to entice last-minute holiday shoppers.

From the grocer's shop came delicious scents of tea and coffee, of cinnamon and sugar and spices.

The poultry shops were still open, with juicy turkeys, squabs, and geese begging to be carried home and eaten for dinner.

Soon the steeple bell called all the good people to church, and the street was filled with them, in their best clothes and their gaiest

A Jolly Time in the Snow

faces. At the same time, from every street and lane came scores of poor people, carrying their dinners to the bakers' shops, for on this day each baker welcomed the poor into his shop to warm their Christmas dinner in his big oven.

As these poor people passed the Spirit and Scrooge, the Spirit lifted the cover of each man's dish and sprinkled incense from his torch on it. But what a strange torch it was. For once or twice when two dinner-carriers bumped into each other and exchanged angry words, the Spirit sprinkled a few drops of water from his torch onto them, and their good spirits returned immediately.

"Is there a particular flavor that you sprinkle from your torch?" asked Scrooge.

"Yes," answered the Spirit. "My own."

"Can that flavor be added to any dinner today?"

"To any," said the Spirit. "But mostly to a poor dinner, for that's the dinner that needs it most."

They continued on, invisible, to the outside

The Spirit Sprinkles Incense.

of town and arrived at the home of Scrooge's clerk, Bob Cratchit. The Spirit stopped at the doorway and blessed the small house with a sprinkling of his torch.

Inside, Mrs. Cratchit, Bob's wife, was setting the table. Her often-mended but clean dress was tied with colorful holiday ribbons. One of her daughters, Belinda, was helping her, while her son, Peter, was dipping a fork into a pan of potatoes to see if they were done.

Two smaller Cratchits, a boy and a girl, came tearing into the room.

"What a delicious smell our noses caught outside the baker's!" cried the boy excitedly.

"It must be our Christmas goose!" added the girl. "I just know it was."

"Where can your dear father be?" asked Mrs. Cratchit. "And your brother, Tiny Tim? They should have been home from church by now. And even your sister Martha is a half-hour late getting here."

The Cratchits Prepare Christmas Dinner.

A Christmas Carol

"I'm here, Mother," called a voice at the doorway.

"Bless your heart, dear Martha!" said Mrs. Crachit, kissing her and taking off her bonnet and shawl. "But how late you are! Was there anything wrong at the milliner's shop?"

"We had a good deal of work to finish last night," said Martha, "and all the apprentices had to clear away this morning."

"Well, it doesn't matter," said Mrs. Cratchit, "as long as you're here. Now sit by the fire and warm up."

"No, no! Father's coming!" cried the two young Cratchits. "Hide, Martha, hide!"

Martha hid behind a closet door, and in came Bob, his threadbare clothes darned but clean. On his shoulders was Tiny Tim, carrying his crutch in the hand that wasn't holding onto his father's neck.

"Why, where's our Martha?" cried Bob, looking around at his family.

"Not coming," said his wife solemnly.

Martha Hides.

A Christmas Carol

"Not coming?" said Bob, suddenly losing his gay spirit. "Not coming home on Christmas Day?"

Martha hated to see her father so disappointed, so she ran out from behind the door and into his arms, while the two Cratchit boys gently eased Tiny Tim down off his father's shoulders and helped him into the kitchen to check on the pudding on the stove.

"And how did little Tiny Tim behave in church?" asked Mrs. Cratchit.

"As good as gold," said Bob. "Sometimes that boy gets the strangest thoughts though! But I guess it's from being alone so much while other children his age are out playing together."

"Why, what were his thoughts, dear?" asked Mrs. Cratchet.

"On the way home from church he told me that he hoped people saw him in church because he was a cripple. When I asked him why, he said it would remind people that on

A Happy Reunion

A Christmas Carol

Christmas Day they should remember their God who made lame beggars walk and blind men see." Bob's voice trembled as he told this to his wife.

Just then, a noisy little crutch was heard on the floor and in came Tiny Tim. His brother and sister helped him get up on his stool by the fire.

Peter and the two young Cratchits then went to bring in the goose and returned in a procession with it. Mrs. Cratchit brought the gravy, while Peter mashed the potatoes, Belinda sweetened the applesauce, and Martha heated the plates.

Bob pulled Tiny Tim's stool to the corner beside him at the table, while the two young Cratchits brought chairs around for everyone.

At last, the family was seated and grace was said.

There was never such a goose—everyone agreed while Mrs. Cratchit was carving. Even though the goose was quite small for

The Family Says Grace.

such a large family, the dinner was filled in with potatoes and applesauce, and not a single morsel was left over.

As Belinda took away the plates, Mrs. Cratchit went to get the pudding.

"Suppose it falls apart?" worried the young Cratchit boy.

"Suppose someone came in and stole it?" said the girl. "That would be worse!"

But in half a minute, Mrs. Cratchit entered, smiling proudly as she held the flaming pudding decorated with a twig of holly on top.

"My dear," said Bob, "this is the best pudding you have made since our marriage."

"I was so worried," she said, sighing with relief. "I wasn't sure it would come out right, for I didn't have enough flour."

Everyone said the pudding was wonderful and not one person mentioned what a small pudding it was for such a large family.

Then all the family gathered in a circle around the hearth. On a small table at Bob's

A Flaming Christmas Pudding

elbow stood all the glasses the family possessed—two tumblers and a cup without a handle. These were filled with a hot mixture of gin and lemons, but it could not have tasted any better if it were served in golden goblets.

As Bob served it, he proposed a toast. "A Merry Christmas to us all, my dears. God bless us!"

The family repeated the toast with Tiny Tim the last of all—"God bless us, everyone!"

Tiny Tim sat very close to his father's side on his little stool. Bob held the boy's withered little hand in his, holding it gently yet tightly, as if he feared that the boy might be taken away from him.

"Spirit," said Scrooge, becoming interested as he had never been before, "tell me if Tiny Tim will live."

"I see an empty stool in the corner and a crutch without an owner. If these shadows of the future, which only I can see, remain

"A Merry Christmas To Us All."

unchanged, that is Tiny Tim's fate!"

"No, no!" cried Scrooge. "Oh, no, kind spirit! Spare him!"

"If these shadows remain unchanged," repeated the Spirit, "he will die.... But why not? After all, you said it would be better if these poor unfortunate creatures died off and decreased the population. You said it yourself. Those were your very words!"

Scrooge hung his head upon hearing the words he had spoken to the two visitors to his warehouse, upon hearing these very same words spoken back to him.

"Man," said the Ghost, "if you are a man in your heart, take back those wicked words. Why should you decide who shall live and who shall die? Perhaps, Heaven will decide that you are less fit to live than this poor man's child!"

Trembling, Scrooge could only stare at the ground, but the sound of his name being called from the shadows caused him to look up.

Scrooge Hears of Tiny Tim's Fate.

A Christmas Carol

"To Mr. Scrooge!" said Bob, raising his tumbler for another toast. "To Mr. Scrooge, who made this feast possible!"

"Mr. Scrooge, indeed!" cried Mrs. Cratchit angrily. "If I had him here, I'd give him a piece of my mind to feast on. Why, Robert, nobody knows better than you what a stingy, hard, hateful, unfeeling old man Mr. Scrooge is!"

"My dear," said Bob calmly, "it is Christmas Day."

"Well," admitted his wife grudgingly, "I'll drink to his health for your sake, Robert, and for the sake of the holiday spirit. But never for Mr. Scrooge's sake!... Long life to Mr. Scrooge! I'm sure he's having a Merry Christmas and a Happy New Year."

The children joined in the toast to Scrooge too, but no one in the family seemed to take much pleasure in doing it. The name of Scrooge darkened everyone's party spirit for a full five minutes. But when it passed, they all

Bob Toasts Mr. Scrooge.

returned to their merry selves, for the Cratchits were a happy family, grateful for what they *did* have and content with each other.

As the scene of the Cratchit family faded into the shadows, Scrooge kept his eyes fixed on Tiny Tim until the last.

As Scrooge and the Spirit went along the streets back to town, it was getting dark and the snow was falling heavily.

The brightness of roaring fires shone from all the windows they passed, with scenes of holiday preparations being made in each house. Ahead of them, children were running out their doors into the snow to greet married sisters, brothers, cousins, uncles, and aunts, and to welcome them to dinner. Guests such as these were entering all the houses along the way.

How the Ghost beamed at the sight of these happy people!

On they went, farther outside town.

Watching Visitors Arrive

A Christmas Carol

Then, suddenly, without a word of warning from the Ghost, Scrooge saw that they had arrived on a bleak and deserted moor. Giant boulders lay on the ground amid frozen moss and coarse grass. In the West, the setting sun shone its last streak of red, while the rest of the sky was filled with the darkest night.

"What kind of place is this?" asked Scrooge.

"A place where miners live," said the Spirit. "These men may labor deep inside the earth, but they still know me. They know the Spirit of Christmas Present! See!" And he pointed to the lighted window of a hut.

Scrooge and the Ghost walked quickly towards it. Passing their invisible selves through the wall of mud and stone, they found a cheerful group around a glowing fire. An old, old man and woman, and their children, their grandchildren and their great-grandchildren, were all decked out in their holiday clothes singing Christmas songs.

A Mining Family Sings Christmas Songs.

A Christmas Carol

The Spirit did not delay here—only long enough for Scrooge to see that here, too, was the spirit of Christmas!

"Take hold of my robe," the Spirit told Scrooge. And they left the house and then the moor. . . high *above* the moor.

Scrooge looked down and back, horrified. "Where are we going?" he cried, as he saw only the roaring sea below and ahead of them.

Then, ahead, on a reef of sunken rocks several miles from shore, stood a lone lighthouse. But even here, the two lighthouse-keepers were sitting at a rough table near a fire, wishing each other a Merry Christmas, while celebrating with their mug of grog.

Again the Spirit and Scrooge sped on, above the black and heaving sea, until they landed on the deck of a ship beside the helmsman at the wheel. The officers and crew were all at their stations, but each man was either humming a Christmas song, or had a Christmas thought, or was talking to his companions

Visiting a Lighthouse

about other Christmases at home.

Then, suddenly, these low voices were interrupted by a hearty laugh. It was with great surprise that Scrooge recognized it as his Nephew's laugh, and it was with even greater surprise that Scrooge found himself in a bright room, with the Spirit at his side.

"Ha, ha!" laughed Scrooge's nephew, Fred. "Ha, ha, ha!" As he laughed, he was rolling his head and making the funniest of faces.

Fred's wife, a pretty young thing with a dimpled face, was laughing too, just as heartily as her husband. And so were their friends, gathered for the holiday at their home.

"And he said," Fred went on, "... he said that Christmas was a humbug! And he believed it too!"

"Shame on him!" said Fred's wife, who was Scrooge's niece by marriage.

"Oh, I don't know," said Fred. "He's a funny

Fred and His Wife Laugh.

old fellow. True, he could be more pleasant, but I have nothing against him."

"You've told me he's very rich," she said.

"What of it, my dear? His wealth is of no use to him. He doesn't do any good with it. He doesn't use it to live comfortably, and he doesn't even have the enjoyment of knowing he is ever going to do any good for us with it."

"Well, I have no patience with him," said the niece. And all the ladies present agreed.

"Oh, I have patience!" said Fred. "I feel sorry for him. I couldn't be angry with him even if I tried. After all, who really suffers by his unpleasant ways? Himself, always. Here's the perfect example. He decided he didn't like us, and so refused our invitation to Christmas dinner. And what's the result? He lost out on a very good dinner. See—it *is* he who suffers."

"Yes, yes!" cried Fred's wife, clapping her hands. "Do go on, Fred."

"I was only going to add that Scrooge missed out on some very pleasant hours and

Discussing Uncle Scrooge

some very pleasant company, and he can't find those in his moldy old office or gloomy apartment. Still, my dear, I plan to invite him every year, whether he likes it or not, for I pity him. He may continue to criticize Christmas as long as he lives, but if I keep going there year after year, in good spirits, who knows—he might even give poor Bob Cratchit a Christmas gift of fifty pounds one day!"

Everyone laughed at that idea, but they laughed, too, because of the good-natured spirit of the holiday.

After tea, the group turned to music. Fred's wife played the harp and everyone sang—a simple little tune which touched Scrooge deeply as he listened, for it was the favorite song years ago of his sister, Fan.

Alphabet games and quiz games followed, with all the guests, young and old, joining in.

For that matter, so did Scrooge, who was so interested that he forgot for the moment

Scrooge Hears an Old, Familiar Song.

that his voice could not be heard as he called out answers to the quizzes.

The Ghost was pleased to see Scrooge like this, but it was now time to go.

"Please," begged Scrooge, "let me stay for just one more game!"

The game was "Yes and No." Fred had to think of something or someone, and the guests had to guess what or who by asking questions that could only be answered by yes or no.

"Yes, it is an animal," answered Fred to the first question. "Yes, a live animal.... Yes, a rather disagreeable animal.... Yes, a savage animal.... Yes, an animal that growled and grunted.... Yes, an animal that even talked sometimes.... Yes, it lived in London and walked about the streets.... No, it wasn't in a show.... No, it wasn't led by anybody.... No, it didn't live in a menagerie.... No, it was never killed in a market.... No, it wasn't a horse... or a cow... or a bull... or a

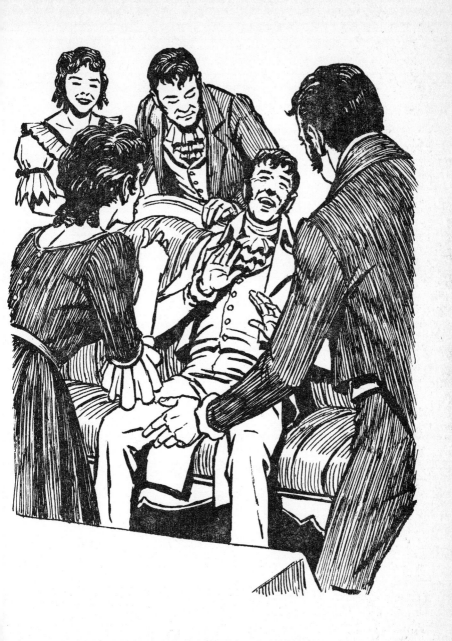

Playing "Yes and No"

tiger. . . or a dog. . . or a hog. . . or a cat. . . or a bear."

With each question, Fred burst into a fresh roar of laughter. He was so delighted and laughed so hard that he had to get up from the sofa and stamp his feet.

At last, one of the ladies, roaring with laughter herself, cried out, "I know what it is, Fred! I've guessed it!"

"What is it?" asked Fred.

"It's your uncle Scro—oo—oge!"

And she was correct!

"But you should have said 'yes' to 'Is it a bear?" one of the guests said to Fred.

"Well, now, my friends," said Fred, "now that Uncle Scrooge has helped us have such a merry time, we must drink a toast to his health!" And lifting his glass, Fred cried, "To Uncle Scrooge!"

"To Uncle Scrooge!" cried the guests. "To Uncle Scrooge's health!"

"A Merry Christmas and a Happy New

"I've Guessed It!"

A Christmas Carol

Year to the old man, wherever he is! added Fred. "He wouldn't take these wishes from me in person, but now he has them, nevertheless. To Uncle Scrooge!"

Uncle Scrooge had become so light-hearted that he was about to thank the guests for their fine toast and wish them a Merry Christmas and a Happy New Year in return. But the Spirit did not give him time. For the entire scene passed away as Scrooge's nephew was uttering his last words. And Scrooge and the Spirit were once again on their way.

They traveled far and they saw much. They visited many homes. They stood beside sick beds suddenly made cheerful for reasons that people couldn't explain. They saw poverty and misery in workhouses, hospitals, and jails, but they left each scene with people a little richer and a little happier with the Spirit's blessings.

It was a long night. What was strange,

"To Uncle Scrooge!"

however, was that while Scrooge did not change in appearance, the Ghost seemed to grow older and older. Scrooge noticed this as the night wore on.

"Are Spirits' lives so short?" he asked.

"My life on earth is very short," said the Ghost. "It ends tonight."

"Tonight at midnight!" answered the Spirit. "Listen now, for my time is drawing near. You must beware of Ignorance and Greed, for they mean DOOM to all mankind . . . unless you and all mankind can change it."

The clock began to strike the hour of twelve.

Scrooge looked around him for the Spirit, but it had gone. As the last stroke resounded, Scrooge remembered Marley's prediction of the third ghost's arrival at the last stroke of midnight. And lifting his eyes, Scrooge saw before him a Phantom, draped and hooded, coming toward him!

The Spirit Gives Scrooge a Warning.

The Ghost of Christmas Yet To Come

CHAPTER 6

The Ghost of Christmas Yet to Come

The Phantom approached Scrooge slowly, gravely. When it came near, it seemed to bring gloom and mystery into the air. The Phantom's body was covered with a dark black robe, which hid its face and its body, and left nothing visible except one outstretched hand.

Scrooge dropped to his knees, but continued staring at the tall, stately Phantom as it stood beside him, speaking not a word!

"Am I in the presence of the Ghost of Christmas Yet To Come?" asked Scrooge.

The Spirit did not answer, but pointed

onward with its hand.

"You are about to show me shadows of things which have not happened yet, but which will happen in the future. Is that correct?" asked Scrooge.

The upper part of the robe that covered the area of the Spirit's head seemed to nod. But this was the only answer it gave Scrooge.

Although he was accustomed to ghostly company by this time, Scrooge was so frightened of the silent shape that his legs trembled beneath him and he could barely stand when he tried to follow the Spirit as it moved onward.

"Oh, Ghost of the Future!" he cried. "I fear you more than any ghost I have ever seen. But I know your purpose is to do good for me. And since I hope to live to be a better man than I was, I am prepared to go with you, and go gratefully. Will you not speak to me?"

The Ghost gave no reply. Its hand was its only answer as it pointed straight ahead.

The Ghost Points Straight Ahead.

"Lead on!" said Scrooge. "The night is passing quickly and the time is precious to me. Lead on, Spirit!"

The Phantom moved away as silently as it had come. Scrooge followed behind its black robe, which seemed to lift him up and carry him along.

The city seemed to spring up all around them—merchants hurrying up and down the streets, talking in groups, looking at their watches, as Scrooge had often seen them do.

The Spirit stopped beside one little group of business men and pointed its hand toward them. Scrooge walked closer to listen to their conversation.

"No," said a big, fat man with a monstrous chin. "I don't know much about it. I only know he's dead."

"When did he die?" asked another.

"Last night, I believe."

"What was the matter with him?" asked a

Scrooge Listens to a Conversation.

third, taking a pinch of snuff out of a very large snuff box. "I thought he'd never die!"

"God only knows what was the matter," said the first man, with a yawn.

"What did he do with his money?" asked a red-faced gentleman with a huge wart on the end of his nose.

"I haven't heard," said the man with the large chin, yawning again. "He probably left it to his company. He hasn't left it to *me*—that much I know!"

At that remark, the group laughed.

"It's probably going to be a cheap funeral," continued the same speaker, "for I certainly don't know of anybody who'd want to go to it. Do you think we should volunteer?"

"I wouldn't mind going if a lunch was served," said the man with a wart. "But I must be fed if I volunteer, especially for *him*!"

Again the group laughed.

"Well," said the first speaker, "I never wear black funeral gloves and I never eat lunch.

The Group Laughs.

But I'll go if any of you do. As a matter of fact, I probably was his only friend, for I was the only one who stopped and spoke to him when we met on the street."

With that, the group broke up, with each gentleman strolling away and joining other groups.

Scrooge looked at the Spirit, surprised that it should have considered such a trivial conversation so important for him to hear.

"But perhaps," Scrooge said to himself, "the Spirit had some hidden purpose. Could the men have been talking about Marley's death? . . . No, that was in the past and this Ghost is the Future. . . . Did I know anybody close to me that could have been the subject of those gentlemen's conversation? . . . No. Well, I'll simply remember all that I have heard," he decided, "and perhaps when I see myself in some of these future shadows, that will give me a clue to why the Spirit had me

Scrooge Is Puzzled.

listen to that conversation."

Scrooge looked about on the street corner and spotted the accustomed place where he had always stood at that time of day. But he couldn't find an image of himself in the crowds. Still, he wasn't surprised, for by now Ebenezer Scrooge had already been making plans to change his entire way of living. "Perhaps," he reasoned, "my not being among these crowds is a sign that I am elsewhere, making a better life for myself."

Then they left the busy business section of the city and went into a remote part of town where Scrooge had never been before. This section had a bad reputation; its narrow streets were dirty and smelly; its shops and houses were broken down; and its people were ugly, drunk, and in rags. The whole section smelled of crime, filth, and misery.

Along one of the narrow streets was a shop that jutted out from the others. From a window Scrooge could see piles and piles of rusty

A Filthy, Miserable Section of Town

keys, chains, hinges, files, scales, weights, and junk iron of all kinds scattered all over the floor. Mountains of dirty rags were heaped everywhere and boxes of bones and animals' insides were crowded together.

Sitting by a charcoal fire among the wares he sold was the owner of the shop—a gray-haired rascal, almost seventy years old. He had hung a curtain of dirty rags on a rope to shield himself from the cold air in the shop. But neither the dirt of the shop nor the cold air seemed to bother him as he sat smoking his pipe luxuriously.

Scrooge and the Phantom entered through the wall just as an old, haggard charwoman came in the door dragging a heavy bundle. She was followed by another woman, also with a bundle, and a man in black. The three were startled to meet there, but they obviously knew each other well, for they all burst into laughter when they got over their surprise.

"I'm first," said the charwoman to Old Joe,

Entering the Junk Shop with Bundles

the shopkeeper. "I was the first to enter the shop. The laundress, there, is second, and the undertaker's helper is third. Now, tell me, Joe, isn't this a coincidence—the three of us meeting here without planning it?"

"Old friends couldn't have met in a better place," said Joe, taking the pipe out of his mouth. "Now, let's all go into the parlor."

The parlor was the screened-off space behind the curtain of rags. Old Joe stirred the coals in the fire with an old stair post, then turned to his customers.

The charwoman threw her bundle on the floor and sat down on a stool, looking defiantly at the other two who had followed her in.

"So you know that I didn't get the goods in this bundle as a gift, don't you, Mrs. Dilbur?" said the charwoman to the laundress.

"Ha!" said Mrs. Dilbur with a sneer.

"Well, every person's got a right to take things," said the charwoman haughtily, "especially when it's to take care of herself.

Old Joe Stirs the Fire

After all, I used to clean and scrub his place. And *him* that I took this stuff from always took care of himself. And *he* won't miss any of it."

"That's true," said the laundress. "I knew him; I did his laundry. And *he* always did make sure to take care of himself . . . never of others."

"And besides," added the charwoman, "who's going to know? *We're* not going to tell on each other."

"No, indeed!" said Mrs. Dilbur and the undertaker's helper together.

"Very well, then!" cried the charwoman. "That's enough. A dead man won't need this stuff."

"No, indeed!" said Mrs. Dilbur, laughing.

"Besides," continued the charwoman, "If he wanted to keep 'em after he was dead, he should have been a better man during his lifetime. If he was, he'd have had somebody to look after him while he was dying, instead

"A Dead Man Won't Need This Stuff."

of lying there, gasping out his last breath all alone."

"That's true," said Mrs. Dilbur. "This is his punishment—having all his belongings stolen."

"It would have been a worse punishment if I could have laid my hands on anything else," said the charwoman.

"All right now," said Old Joe. "Let's get down to business. I'll take the smallest bundle first."

The undertaker's helper opened his first. There wasn't much in it—a pencil case, a few buttons, and a brooch of little value.

Old Joe examined the loot carefully and noted the price he would pay for each on the wall. Then he added them up. "This is all I'll pay," he said, pointing to the total on the wall. "This . . . not another penny. Now, who's next?"

Mrs. Dilbur, the laundress, opened her bundle next. It contained sheets, towels, a

Old Joe Adds Up the Prices.

few pieces of clothing, a pair of boots, and a pair of sugar tongs.

Joe added up their value on the wall the same way he did the undertaker's helper's loot and announced the total to Mrs. Dilbur. "I'm being very generous," he added. "I always have a weakness when I do business with ladies."

"Now undo *my* bundle, Joe," said the charwoman.

Joe got down on his knees and had to open a great many knots before he was able to lift out a large, heavy roll of some dark cloth.

"What are these?" he asked. "Bed-curtains?"

"Yes!" exclaimed the woman. "Bed-curtains!"

"Do you mean to say you took 'em down, rings and all, with him lying there?"

"Yes," replied the woman. "Why not? I'm certainly not going to keep my hands in my pockets if I can get something of value in them just

Mrs. Dilbur's Bundle

by reaching out ... especially from a man like *him*! Look, there! There's blankets too!"

"*His* blankets?" asked Joe.

"Who else's did you think?" she replied with a sneer. "He isn't likely to catch cold without them."

Everyone laughed at that!

Old Joe was now holding a man's finely woven silk shirt up to the light.

"You can look all you want to, Joe," said the charwoman. "Look till your eyes hurt. But you won't find a hole in that shirt, or a patch, or a worn spot. It was his best shirt ... and it would have been wasted if it hadn't been for me."

"What do you mean 'wasted'?" asked Joe.

"Somebody had put it on him to be buried in," she said with a laugh. "That was a fool thing to do, so I took it off him and put on an old cotton one instead. His body looked just as good—or just as ugly—in the cotton one as it did in the fine silk one!"

"It Was His Best Shirt."

A Christmas Carol

When Old Joe handed her a flannel bag with money in it, the charwoman laughed. "Ha, ha! This is the result of his life, you see! He frightened us all away from him when he was alive, but we're making a profit on him now that he is dead! Ha, ha, ha!"

"Spirit!" cried Scrooge with a shudder. "This unhappy man they're talking about could have been me, for I have been leading just that kind of life they described. . . . But merciful Heavens! What is this?"

Scrooge drew back in terror, for the scene had changed. Now he was standing beside a bed—a bare bed with no curtains and no blankets. On the bed, beneath a ragged sheet, lay something very silent and unmoving. No one was in the room with the body to watch over it. . . to weep over it. . . or to care for it.

Scrooge glanced cautiously towards the Phantom. Its hand was pointing to the head of the body, as if telling Scrooge to lift the

The Phantom Points to the Head.

ragged sheet and reveal the face. But Scrooge couldn't move. His arms seemed to have lost the power to raise even anything as light as the ragged sheet.

Scrooge looked up at the Phantom, his eyes filled with tears. "Spirit!" he cried. "I have learned a lesson in this fearful house of death . . . a lesson I shall never forget. Let us go now!"

But the Spirit did not move, only stood there with its finger pointed at the head beneath the sheet.

"I understand what you are telling me," said Scrooge. "I would uncover this face if I could. But my arms do not have the power to raise it."

The Phantom seemed to gaze at Scrooge from the blackness, but still it did not move.

"Please, Spirit, if there is any person in this town who feels *any* emotion over this man's death," cried Scrooge in agony, "show that person to me. I beg you!"

"I Have Learned a Lesson!"

A Christmas Carol

The Phantom spread its dark robe in front of Scrooge, and when it pulled the robe back, a mother and her small children appeared.

The mother seemed anxious, as if she was expecting someone, for she was pacing back and forth, glancing at the clock, stopping at the window, and jumping with each sound into the house.

Finally, the long-expected knock came, and she hurried to the door to let her husband in. He was a young man, though his face was troubled and weary.

His wife led him to a table set with his dinner and waited patiently for him to speak.

After a long silence, during which the young man did not even lift his fork, his wife finally forced herself to speak.

"Do you have news?" she asked.

The young man seemed embarrassed as to how to answer her. "Y-yes," he said quietly. "But it is bad."

An Anxious Mother Paces.

A Christmas Carol

"Are we ruined?" she asked fearfully.

"Not yet, Caroline," replied her husband. "There is still a bit of hope."

"If *he* has agreed to extend our loan, then there is hope," she said. "But that would be a miracle to expect *him* to agree ... Yet, has such a miracle happened?"

"He is past agreeing, my dear. He is dead!"

The young woman gasped—first thankful that *he* was dead ... then praying forgiveness for her thoughts.

Her husband went on to explain. "I checked out everything today, for last night when I tried to see him to beg for a week's extension in making the payment, I met a drunken charwoman coming out of his apartment. When she told me that he was very ill—dying, in fact—I thought he was using that as an excuse to avoid me. But I found out this morning that what she told me was true. For he *is* dead."

"Are We Ruined?"

A Christmas Carol

"But what about our debt?" asked Caroline. "Will it be transferred to another person? And will we have to pay him?"

"I don't know," said the young man. "But before that happens, I'm certain that we'll have the money. And even if we do not, the person who takes over our debt would certainly have to be kinder than *he* was. No one could be as merciless as he was to us. So, my dear Caroline, we can sleep tonight with our hearts just a little bit lighter."

The hearts of the young couple were lighter and even their children, now quiet and trying to understand what their parents were saying, seemed more cheerful as they saw their parents finally smile. Yes, this was a happier house as a result of *that man's* death!

"Spirit," said Scrooge. "You have shown me a scene of pleasure at a man's death. Is there no one who still feels sorrow over death? Do people no longer mourn over death? I must

A Happier House

see that people still do mourn over each other, or that terrible deathbed scene will remain with me forever."

The Spirit led Scrooge through several familiar streets. As they went along, Scrooge looked all around, hoping to catch a glimpse of himself in this future world. But he was nowhere to be seen!

They stopped next at Bob Cratchit's house—a place Scrooge had visited with the Ghost of Christmas Present. Mrs. Cratchit and her daughters were seated around the fire, busy sewing on some coarse black cloth. Everyone was quiet. Even the noisy little Cratchits were as still as statues as they sat in one corner looking up at Master Peter, who was reading to them in very low tones.

As Scrooge and the Phantom crossed the threshold, Scrooge heard Peter's soft words, muffled with sobs.

"And he took a child, and set him in the

Everyone Is Quiet.

midst of them."

But the boy couldn't go on. He stopped reading, for his tears had all but choked him.

Mrs. Cratchit put down her sewing and covered her face with her hands. Through her tears, she tried to reassure her children, "It's the sewing, my dears. Sewing on this black cloth hurts my eyes."

"Oh, no!" cried Scrooge. "Poor Tiny Tim! Is he . . .?"

And the Phantom seemed to nod from the blackness.

"My eyes are better now," said Mrs. Cratchit to her children after a few moments. "You see, my dears, working by candlelight weakens them and makes them red. And I don't want your father to see them red when he comes home. He should be here shortly."

"It's past time, Mother," said Peter, shutting the book. "But Father has been walking

Mrs. Cratchit Is In Tears.

slower these last few evenings...slower than he used to."

Then they were quiet again.

After several minutes, Mrs. Cratchit felt herself steadier, and in a more cheerful voice she said, "Why, I have seen your father walk very fast, even with...even with Tiny Tim on his shoulders."

"So have I!" cried Peter. "Often!"

"And so have I!" cried the other children.

"But Tiny Tim was very light to carry," continued Mrs. Cratchit as she picked up her sewing again. "And his father loved him so much that it was no trouble...no trouble... Oh, listen! Your father is at the door."

Mrs. Cratchit hurried out to meet her husband and bring him into the room where she had his tea ready for him.

As the older children tried to be first to serve their father his tea, the two Cratchits climbed up on his lap and each laid a cheek against his face, as if to say,

Bringing Bob Into the Room

A Christmas Carol

"Don't grieve, Father."

Bob Cratchit tried to be cheerful with his family and spoke pleasantly to them. He praised his wife's sewing and his daughters' as well.

"You have all worked quickly," he told them. "I'm sure these clothes will be ready to wear Sunday."

"Sunday?" asked his wife. "You mean you have made the arrangements for the funeral Sunday?"

"Yes, my dear," said Bob gently. "I went there today. I wish you could have gone too. It would have done you good to see how green and peaceful the place is. But you'll see it often. I promised him that I would walk there on Sundays. . . . Oh, my little child! My little child!"

Bob could no longer hold back his tears. And he wept for several minutes while his family looked on, helpless, unable to console him.

"Oh, My Little Child!"

A Christmas Carol

He left the room and went upstairs into a room that was cheerfully lit and hung with Christmas decorations. A chair was placed near a tiny coffin. Bob sat down and looked at the tiny, peaceful figure. Then he leaned over and kissed Tiny Tim's silent lips.

More composed now and feeling better for having shared that moment with his son, Bob went downstairs and rejoined his family around the fire.

"I met Mr. Scrooge's nephew today," he told them. "You know, I had only seen him once or twice before, but he seemed to sense that something was wrong, for he commented that I looked a bit down, and asked me why. Then, when I explained about our beloved Tiny Tim, he was just the kindest man ever. He said how sorry he was about our loss and so sorry for our entire family."

"That was kind of him," said Mrs. Cratchit.

"And then," continued Bob, "he gave me his

Sharing a Moment with His Son

card and said, 'If I can be of any service to you in any way, here is where I live. Please do not hesitate to come to me.' Oh, he was so kind. It really seemed as if he had known our Tiny Tim and felt our grief with us."

"I'm sure he's a good soul," said Mrs. Cratchit.

"And I wouldn't be surprised—mark my words!—if he even tried to get our Peter a better job."

"Do you hear that, Peter?" exclaimed Mrs. Cratchit.

"And then Peter will find a girl," said Belinda, "and get married and. . . ."

"Get along with you!" cried Peter, grinning.

"There's plenty of time for that one of these days," said Bob. "We will all part from one another one day when all of you children are grown and married and with your own families, but I'm sure that none of us will ever forget poor Tiny Tim. . . and none of us will

An Offer of Kindness

ever forget this first time that there has been a parting among us."

"We shall never forget, Father!" cried the children.

"And I know," said Bob, "I know, my dears, that when we recall how good and patient that little child was, we shall stop and think twice before we quarrel among ourselves."

"Yes, Father!" they all cried. "We shall."

"Then I shall be very happy," said Bob. "Very happy!"

Mrs. Cratchit kissed him; his daughters kissed him; the two young Cratchits kissed him; and Peter went out to him and shook his hand.

This, then, was the beautiful influence of the memory of Tiny Tim.

"Spirit," said Scrooge, "I am getting the feeling that our time to part is very close. Tell me, now, I beg of you, who that dead

The Beautiful Influence of Tiny Tim

man was."

The Ghost of Christmas Yet To Come carried Scrooge along sometime in the Future, into the courtyard of the Scrooge and Marley Warehouse.

"This is my place of business," said Scrooge. "I see the building even now. Let me see myself as I will be in the days to come."

The Spirit stopped, its hand pointing away in another direction.

"My warehouse is *here!*" exclaimed Scrooge. "Why are you pointing elsewhere?"

The finger did not move, but continued pointing away.

Scrooge rushed to the window of his office and looked in. "It is still an office," he said, "but not mine. The furniture is different and the figure in the chair is not me."

Still the Phantom's finger pointed as before.

Scrooge took hold of the Spirit's robe, and they were gone again. They stopped when

"The Figure in the Chair Is Not Me."

they reached an iron gate.

Scrooge paused to look around before he opened the gate. "It's a churchyard!" he exclaimed. "And underneath its ground lays the wretched man whose name I have been trying to learn. But what a wretched place this is! Closed in by houses! Overrun with weeds! Crowded with graves upon graves! Truly a worthy place for such a wretched man!"

The Spirit moved among the graves and pointed down towards one.

Scrooge approached it, trembling. Although the Phantom stood unmoving, Scrooge dreaded the new meaning he suddenly found in its deathlike shape.

"Before I draw closer to that stone you are pointing at, Spirit," said Scrooge fearfully, "answer me one question. Are the shadows you have shown me scenes of things that *will* be, or are they only scenes of things that *may* be?"

Still, the Spirit pointed downward to the

The Spirit Points Toward One Grave.

grave.

"A man's life may lead him to certain ends," said Scrooge, "but if he changes the course of his life, will those ends change as well? Please tell me that this is so, for I fear what you are about to show me!"

Still the Spirit did not move.

Scrooge crept toward the grave, trembling as he followed the finger. Reaching the stone of the neglected grave, he read the name on the stone—EBENEZER SCROOGE!

"Am *I* that man who lay upon the bed?" he cried, looking up beseechingly at the Spirit.

The finger pointed from the grave to him and back again.

"No, Spirit! Oh, no, no!"

The finger was still pointing to the grave.

"Spirit!" cried Scrooge, clutching at its robe. "Hear me! I am not the man I was. I will not be that wretched creature any longer. Am I past all hope? Is this why you are showing me all this?"

"No, Spirit! Oh, No, No!"

A Christmas Carol

For the first time, the Spirit's hand appeared to shake.

"Good Spirit," pleaded Scrooge, "your good nature must have pity on me. Assure me that I can still change my life!"

The Spirit's hand trembled.

"I will honor Christmas in my heart," promised Scrooge, "and I will try to keep its spirit all year. I will live in the Past, the Present, and the Future. I will not forget the lessons that the Spirits of all three have taught me. Oh, please, tell me that I may erase the writing on this stone!"

In his agony, Scrooge reached out and caught at the Spirit's hand. But the Spirit was stronger than Scrooge and pulled its hand free.

Holding up his hands in one last prayer to have his fate changed, Scrooge suddenly saw the Phantom's hood and robe shrink. It continued to shrink and shrink until it finally collapsed into a bedpost!

"Your Good Nature Must Have Pity on Me."

Only the Bedpost Is There.

CHAPTER 7

Christmas Day

Yes. Only the bedpost was there—Scrooge's own bedpost in his own room. Best of all, the time was his own—time for Scrooge to made amends.

"I will live in the Past, the Present, and the Future!" vowed Scrooge. And he repeated those words over and over, as he happily scrambled out of bed. "Oh, Jacob Marley! Oh, Heaven and Christmas time! Praised be to you all for this—for my second chance. I say it on my knees, old Jacob, on my knees!"

Scrooge was sobbing now, but glowing

happily in his sobbing. His face was wet with tears.

"They are not torn down!" he cried, folding one of the bed-curtains in his arms. "They are not torn down, rings and all. They are here. I am here. The shadows of things to come may still be changed. They will be. I know they will!"

Scrooge's hands were busy with his clothes as he rushed to get dressed. In his joyous excitement, he was turning his clothes inside out, putting them on upside down, tearing them, dropping them.

"I don't know what to do!" he cried, laughing and crying in the same breath. "I am as light as a feather! I am as happy as an angel! I am as merry as a schoolboy! I am as giddy as a drunken man! A Merry Christmas to everybody! A Happy New Year to all the world! Hallo! Whoopee!"

Scrooge had skipped into his sitting-room and was now standing there, out of breath.

"They Are Not Torn Down!"

A Christmas Carol

"There's my saucepan of broth still on the fireplace ledge!" he cried, skipping around again, overjoyed to see things as they were. "There's the door by which the Ghost of Jacob Marley entered! There's the corner where the Ghost of Christmas Present sat! There's the window through which I saw the wandering, crying spirits! It's all true! It all happened! Ha, ha, ha!"

For a man who had not had so much practice laughing for so many years, Scrooge's laugh was a splendid one, a brilliant one!

"I don't know what day of the month it is," he said. "I don't know how long I have been among the Spirits. I don't know anything. I'm a baby. Never mind. I don't care. I'd rather be a baby. Hallow! Whoopee!"

Scrooge was stopped for a moment in his bounding leaps by the church bells ringing out the loudest, happiest peals he had ever heard. "Ding, dong, bell!" Scrooge repeated with them in chorus. "Bell, dong, ding! Clang,

Overjoyed To See Things As They Were

clash! Oh, glorious bells!"

Then running to the window, Scrooge opened it and stuck his head out. "The fog is gone!" he said happily. "The mist is gone! It is a clear, bright, happy, cold day. Cold enough to make my blood dance and dance gaily. Oh, golden sunlight, how you are shining! Oh, heavenly sky! Oh, sweet fresh air! Oh, merry bells! Oh, glorious, glorious life!"

Then, seeing a boy below dressed in Sunday clothes, Scrooge called down, "Tell me, lad, what day is today?"

"Huh?" answered the boy in surprise.

"What day is today, my fine fellow?" repeated Scrooge.

"Today?" replied the boy. "Why, it's Christmas Day!"

"It's Christmas Day!" whispered Scrooge joyously. "I haven't missed it after all. The Spirits did it all in one night. They can do anything they like. Of course they can!"

Then Scrooge leaned out the window again,

"Today? Why It's Christmas Day!"

calling, "Hallo there, my fine fellow! Do you know the poultry shop at the corner of the next street?"

"Yes, sir. Of course," answered the boy.

"An intelligent lad!" said Scrooge, smiling. "In fact, a remarkable boy! . . . Tell me, lad, do you know if they've sold the prize turkey that's been hanging up in the window? Not the little one— the big one?"

"You mean the one as big as me?" asked the boy.

"What a delightful boy!" exclaimed Scrooge. "What a pleasure to talk to him! . . . Yes, my lad, that's the one I mean."

"It's hanging there now, sir," answered the boy.

"Good!" cried Scrooge. "Go and buy it!"

"You're joking!" exclaimed the boy.

"No, no," said Scrooge. "I am serious. Go and buy it and tell 'em to bring it here and I'll give 'em directions where to take it. Go now, boy. And come back with the poultry man and

"Go and Buy It!"

A Christmas Carol

I'll give you a shilling for your trouble. In fact, lad, if you come back with him in less than five minutes, I'll give you half a crown!"

The boy took off like a shot!

"I'll send it to Bob Cratchit's," whispered Scrooge, rubbing his hands in anticipation and splitting his sides with laughter. "And he shan't know who sent it. Why, that turkey's twice the size of Tiny Tim! What a fine joke this will be!"

Scrooge set about writing the Cratchits' address on a piece of paper. His hand was not very steady after all he had been through, but write it he did! Then he rushed downstairs and to the door to wait for the poultry man.

As Scrooge stood there waiting for him to arrive, the large door knocker caught his eye. "I shall love you as long as I live," he cried, patting the knocker lovingly. "I hardly ever looked at you before, knocker. What an honest expression you have on your face! You're a wonderful knocker! . . . Oh, here's the turkey.

"What a Fine Joke This Will Be!"

Hallo! How are you? Merry Christmas!"

And what a turkey it was! Scrooge couldn't see how the bird ever could have stood on its legs, for its body was so huge!

"Why, it's impossible to carry that turkey all the way to that part of town where the Cratchits live," Scrooge told the poultry man. "You must take a cab."

Scrooge chuckled as he said this, and chuckled as he paid for the turkey, and chuckled when he paid for the cab, and chuckled when he tipped the boy. But the loudest chuckle came when he sat down, breathless, in his chair and chuckled till he cried.

Shaving was next—not an easy task for Scrooge, as his hand continued to shake, since he was dancing as he was doing it. But if he had cut off the end of his nose, he would have put a piece of bandage over it and quite forgotten about it.

He dressed himself in his best clothes and

What a Turkey It Is!

went down into the street. By now, people were walking about, as he had seen them do with the Ghost of Christmas Present.

Walking with his hands behind him, Scrooge looked at everyone with a delighted smile. He looked so pleasant, in fact, that three or four jovial men said, "Good morning, sir! A Merry Christmas to you!"

Scrooge was to say later that of all the happy sounds he had ever heard, those were the happiest to his ears!

He had not gone far when he saw approaching him the stout gentleman who, with his associate, had visited his warehouse yesterday to request a donation for charity. "Oh, dear!" thought Scrooge. "What must that old gentleman think of me! I must change that opinion immediately!"

So Scrooge quickened his steps until he was face to face with the man. "My dear sir," he said, taking the startled gentleman by both hands. "How do you do? I hope you were

A Delighted Smile for Everyone!

successful yesterday. I hope you collected much money for the poor. It was so kind of you to give your time for this noble effort! A Merry Christmas to you, sir!"

"Mr. Scrooge?" asked the man, bewildered. "Are you the same Mr. Scrooge I called on yesterday?"

"Yes," answered Scrooge, "that is my name, although I fear you might not think too highly of it. Please let me ask your pardon and will you accept. . . . " And Scrooge whispered in the old gentleman's ear.

"Lord bless me!" cried the gentleman, as he gasped for breath. "My dear Mr. Scrooge, are you serious?"

"Yes," said Scrooge, "and not a shilling less! This includes a great many back payments that I missed. Now, will you accept it?"

"My dear sir," said the gentleman, shaking hands with Scrooge, "I don't know what to say to such generosity! Why I—"

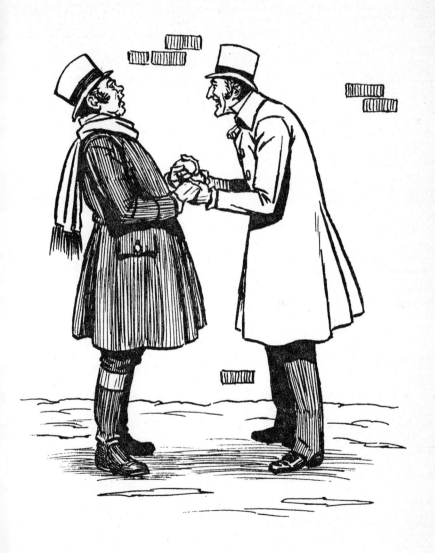

"My Dear Mr. Scrooge, Are You Serious?"

A Christmas Carol

"Don't say anything, please," interrupted Scrooge. "Just come and see me from time to time when you are nearby. Will you?"

"I will!" cried the old gentleman. And he really meant it.

"Thank you," said Scrooge. "And God bless you!"

Scrooge spent the rest of that Christmas morning in a most remarkable way—a way he had never done before. He went to church, then walked about the streets. He watched people hurrying to and fro; he patted children on the head; he talked to beggars; he looked into windows of houses and took pleasure in seeing happy people enjoying the holiday. Everything he did, everything he saw gave him pleasure. He had never dreamed that any walk—that anything—could bring him so much happiness.

In the afternoon, Scrooge turned his steps to his nephew's house. But when he reached the door, he walked past it a dozen times

Scrooge Goes to Church.

before he got up the courage to knock. Finally, he made a dash to the door and knocked.

A smiling young housemaid answered the door.

"Is your master at home, my dear?" asked Scrooge.

"Yes, sir."

"Where is he, my dear?"

"In the dining room, sir, along with the mistress. I'll show you in and announce you, sir."

"Thank you," said Scrooge, with his hand already on the dining room door knob. "He knows me. I'll go right in."

Scrooge turned the knob gently and peeked his face around the slightly open door. His niece and nephew were standing admiring their beautifully set holiday dinner table, making certain that everything was ready for their guests when they arrived.

"Fred!" called Scrooge.

"Why, bless my soul!" cried Fred. "Who is it?"

Admiring a Holiday Dinner Table

A Christmas Carol

"It is I, your Uncle Scrooge. I have come to dinner. Will you let me in?"

"Let you in!" cried Fred, rushing up to Scrooge and shaking his hand so hard and so long, that it seemed to Scrooge his hand might fall off.

It took no more than five minutes and Uncle Scrooge was feeling right at home. Nothing could have made him happier.

Then the guests came—all those guests Scrooge had seen when he was with the Ghost of Christmas Present. And they all looked the same as they did in the Spirit's shadows.

It was a wonderful party, with all the music and all the games Scrooge had only been able to hear and watch earlier. Now he was part of them—part of the wonderful friendly spirit, part of the wonderful gaiety, part of the wonderful happiness!

Uncle Scrooge Feels Right at Home.

Scrooge Is at His Office Early.

CHAPTER 8

A New Boss for Bob

Early the next morning Scrooge arrived at his office early. He had his heart set on being there especially early. . . and even catching Bob Cratchit coming in late.

And he did. Yes, he did! The clock struck nine. No Bob. A quarter past nine. No Bob.

"He's now eighteen and a half minutes late," said Scrooge with a grin as he sat at his desk with the door open so he could watch for this clerk.

Suddenly, the outer door burst open and in one movement, Bob Cratchit removed his hat and scarf, and was on his stool, pen in hand.

"Hallo!" growled Scrooge, trying hard to use his former harsh voice. "What do you mean by strolling in here at this hour of the day?"

"I'm very sorry, sir," said Bob, as his pen was speedily scratching away. "I know I'm late."

"Yes, I think you are," said Scrooge. "Come into my office immediately!"

"It only happened once, sir," pleaded Bob, as he appeared at the door to Scrooge's office. "It won't happen again, sir. I promise. It was only because of the holiday celebration yesterday, sir."

"I'm not going to stand for this sort of thing any longer," growled Scrooge as he leaped down from his stool with his ruler in his hand and came face to face with Cratchit. "And so," added Scrooge, pounding his ruler into the young man's chest and forcing him to back out of the office, "so I am going to raise your salary!"

Coming Face to Face with Cratchit

A Christmas Carol

Bob trembled and took a few timid steps toward the ruler. He had the momentary idea of grabbing that ruler and knocking Scrooge down with it and holding the old man on the floor while he called for the police to bring a straitjacket—for surely Scrooge had lost his mind!

"A Merry Christmas, Bob!" said Scrooge. And his voice was so sincere that Bob could no longer doubt that the old man really meant what he said.

Bob smiled, but still could not speak as Scrooge slapped him on the back and repeated his Christmas wishes.

"A Merrier Christmas, my good fellow, than I have ever given you in many years!" said Scrooge, smiling. "Not only am I raising your salary, but I am going to try to help your struggling family too."

Bob still stood frozen in amazement, and could only nod and smile.

"Yes, Bob," continued Scrooge, "we will

Has Scrooge Lost His Mind?

discuss all these things this very afternoon over a Christmas drink of hot port wine. We'll talk about an apprenticeship for Master Peter, and see what doctors we can find to help Tiny Tim. We'll scour the entire world if we have to, but we'll find someone who can do something for that angel of a boy!" "Y-yes, sir!" exclaimed Bob, sobbing. "Th-thank you, sir!"

"And, Bob," added Scrooge, "let's raise the fire and get more heat in here. In fact, hurry out right now and buy another coal bucket to keep in your office, and lots more coal as well. And do it before you dot another *i* with your pen, Bob Cratchit!"

"Let's Raise the Fire."

A Good Boss

CHAPTER 9

The New Ebenezer Scrooge

Scrooge kept his word. He did everything he promised and more... much more.

To Tiny Tim, who did not die and who even walked again without his crutches, Scrooge became a second father.

He became as good a friend, as good a boss, and as good a citizen as the old city—or any other city in the world—had ever known.

Some people laughed to see the change in him, but Scrooge let them laugh, for he knew that nothing good ever happened in this world that some people did not laugh at, at first.

A Christmas Carol

What was more important to Scrooge, was that his own heart was laughing—laughing with joy at giving and helping others.

Ebenezer Scrooge had no further meetings with the Spirits, but still he continued to live a good life. People soon began to say of him that *he* truly knew the meaning of the spirit of Christmas, perhaps better than any man alive. And he lived with that spirit not only at Christmas time, but all during the year.

And Ebenezer Scrooge's words, for the rest of his long and happy life, were Tiny Tim's words—"God bless us, everyone!"

"God Bless Us, Everyone!"